Trick or Treat or Trap?

While Nan and Bert peered at the Greek vases, Freddie quietly slipped back into the mummy's room.

A lone spotlight was focused on the open casket. The room was dead quiet.

Freddie tiptoed to the edge of the casket and peeked in. Phew! Mummies really smelled musty.

Freddie leaned forward to touch the ragged bandages, and then he froze. The bandaged chest moved. Up, then down, then up again. The mummy was breathing!

Freddie tried to yell, but no sound came out. Then, before he could turn and run, the mummy's arms reached out to grab him!

Books in The New Bobbsey Twins series

\# 1 The Secret of Jungle Park
\# 2 The Case of the Runaway Money
\# 3 The Clue That Flew Away
\# 4 The Secret in the Sand Castle
\# 5 The Case of the Close Encounter
\# 6 Mystery on the Mississippi
\# 7 Trouble in Toyland
\# 8 The Secret of the Stolen Puppies
\# 9 The Clue in the Classroom
\#10 The Chocolate-covered Clue
\#11 The Case of the Crooked Contest
\#12 The Secret of the Sunken Treasure
\#13 The Case of the Crying Clown
\#14 The Mystery of the Missing Mummy

Available from MINSTREL Books

THE NEW
Bobbsey
Twins™

#14
THE MYSTERY OF THE MISSING MUMMY

LAURA LEE HOPE
ILLUSTRATED BY PAUL JENNIS

A MINSTREL® BOOK

PUBLISHED BY POCKET BOOKS

New York   London   Toronto   Sydney   Tokyo

A MINSTREL PAPERBACK *ORIGINAL*

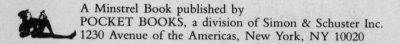 A Minstrel Book published by
POCKET BOOKS, a division of Simon & Schuster Inc.
1230 Avenue of the Americas, New York, NY 10020

ISBN: 0-671-67595-8

First Minstrel Books printing October 1989

10 9 8 7 6 5 4 3 2 1

Contents

1. The Mummy Moves   1
2. A Living Legend   13
3. Halloween Revelry   22
4. Hidden Treasure   30
5. Secrets in the Leaves   37
6. Trick-or-Treat Terror   44
7. On the Mummy Watch   53
8. A Muddy Trail   62
9. The Big Shadow   71
10. Mummy to the Rescue   78

1

The Mummy Moves

"Boo!" A ghostly figure leapt out from behind the red brick chimney in the Bobbsey family's attic. But it was no ghost. It was only Freddie Bobbsey with a white sheet slung over his head.

Flossie Bobbsey made a face at her twin brother. "You can't frighten me," she said. "Even if it is almost Halloween."

Flossie tugged a short black glove onto one hand. It just covered her wrist.

"These fit perfectly," she cried. "Now all I need is a tail and some pointed ears, and I'll look exactly like a black cat." With her black leotard, black tights, and little black gloves, her costume was finally coming together.

"I don't want to be a ghost, anyway." Freddie pulled the sheet off his blond head. "I want to go as something *really* scary this year."

"Just be yourself," Flossie teased. "That's plenty scary."

"How's this?" Bert, their twelve-year-old brother, pulled a Frankenstein mask and one of his father's old jackets out of a dusty trunk. "I'll wear my football pads under the shoulders." He slipped into the jacket and held the Frankenstein mask over his face.

"I thought you were going as Rex Sleuther, private eye," Flossie said. Her older brother was the comic-book hero's biggest fan in Lakeport.

"No, I went as Rex Sleuther last year." Bert smiled. "Remember?" He hunched his shoulders and turned up the collar of the jacket, imitating the detective on a stakeout. "Boy, did I look tough."

"Heee, heee, heee!" Shrill laughter rang through the attic, startling Freddie and Flossie.

"Double, double, toil and trouble!" Nan, Bert's twin, cackled in a scratchy voice as she stepped out of the shadows under the eaves. A pointed black witch's hat nearly covered her

2

brown hair. She also wore a rubber mask of a wrinkled face with a crooked, warty nose.

"Now, that's scary," Flossie said, her blue eyes wide.

"Didn't scare me," Freddie insisted, even though everyone had seen him jump.

"Just practicing." Nan pulled the mask off her face. "Every witch needs a wicked laugh." She cast an eerie smile at her younger brother. "What are you going to be?"

"I don't know yet, but I'll think of something." Halloween was only two days away, and Freddie still didn't have a costume. But thanks to the local teachers' convention, all the students in Lakeport had two extra days off from school. Two whole days! Freddie would need every minute of that time to get a costume together.

Just then the twins heard footsteps on the creaking attic stairs.

"Where are you?" The voice echoed faintly. Everyone froze as the attic door slid open, creaking loudly.

But the woman in the doorway didn't look spooky at all. It was Mrs. Bobbsey, the twins' mother. She laughed at their surprised faces. "You all look as if you've just seen a ghost."

"It's a creepy time of year," Bert said. He pulled on the Frankenstein mask and growled.

"My son the monster." Mrs. Bobbsey chuckled. "How's the costume search going?"

"I'm almost all set," Flossie said. She fished a long black scarf out of the trunk and held it behind her as if it were a tail. "Trick or treat!"

Mrs. Bobbsey laughed. "Well, I don't know if I'm in the mood for a trick. How about a treat?"

"Yeah!" the Bobbseys cheered.

"Here's what it is," their mother said. "The *Lakeport News* has asked me to write a story about a new exhibit at the museum."

Mrs. Bobbsey was a part-time reporter for their hometown newspaper. "How would you like to go see an Egyptian mummy?"

"A real live mummy?" Flossie's mouth dropped open.

"Mummies aren't alive," Freddie scoffed. He looked at his mother. "Are they?"

Mrs. Bobbsey explained that Egyptian mummies were dead bodies preserved by special chemicals and wrapped in bandages. "They can be thousands of years old," she added.

"Sounds spooky," said Flossie with a shiver.

"They can't hurt you," Bert said. "Except in the movies. Sounds like a good idea, Mom. Let's go."

"Wait a minute," said Mrs. Bobbsey. "Let me look at your costumes. Let's see. Nan's a witch, Bert is Frankenstein, the glamorous black cat is Flossie, and Freddie's a—"

"Mummy!" Freddie shouted. "That's what I'll be. A mummy!"

"You don't even know what a mummy looks like," Nan pointed out.

"No," Freddie replied, "but anything a thousand years old must be totally gross and creepy! Just right for me."

The cool marble halls of the Lakeport Museum echoed with the Bobbseys' footsteps.

"Don't wander off," Mrs. Bobbsey said to the twins. "The museum is closed tonight— except for a few special visitors like us."

Mr. Foxworth, the museum curator, led the way. He was a middle-aged man with a beard.

"Where's the mummy?" Freddie whispered.

"There, in that exhibit hall." Bert pointed ahead of them.

A bright light shone in a room at the end of the dimly lit hall. The mummy exhibit looked just like the inside of an Egyptian tomb. Pictures were etched into its stone walls, and the room was lined with statues of people and animals.

In the center of the tomb sat a long stone box carved in the shape of a man lying down. The lid had been slid open a bit.

"That's the sarcophagus," Nan whispered. "The mummy's inside that box."

"That's right," said Mr. Foxworth. "The ancient Egyptians believed the dead lived on in another world. So they thought their bodies should be preserved forever, along with their most valued possessions. Their tombs were also filled with statues of their servants."

"The servants were supposed to work for their masters in the afterlife, too," Nan added.

Mr. Foxworth nodded, impressed with Nan's knowledge. He pointed at the painted face on the stone casket. "That's what the mummy looked like when he was alive. His name was King Am-ho-tep."

"Wow." Freddie craned his neck to look closer. The king's long black hair was braided and entwined with shiny red, blue, and green beads. His gold robes were decorated with pictures of birds.

Freddie turned toward the sketches of birds, cats, and people that covered the tomb's walls.

"Those are hieroglyphics," Nan said.

"Hi-row-what?" Flossie asked.

"Hieroglyphics. It's a kind of writing, sort of like a secret code."

While the Bobbseys studied the ancient drawings, two more people entered the room.

"Ah, there you are." Mr. Foxworth introduced the Bobbseys to Mrs. Truesdale, a large woman wearing a thick fur cape. "Mrs. Truesdale is the mummy's owner," Mr. Foxworth explained. "She loaned it to us for this special exhibit."

"This is my nephew, Lex," Mrs. Truesdale said, putting her arm around a short, thin boy beside her. He looked about fifteen.

The teenager seemed very uncomfortable. His eyes darted nervously to the mummy's stone casket as though he were afraid of it. When Mr. Foxworth proudly patted the sarcophagus, Lex flinched as though he thought the box would explode.

Mrs. Bobbsey opened her notebook. "How long will Am-ho-tep be on display?" she asked.

"Two weeks," Mr. Foxworth answered.

Behind them, Nan studied the hiero-glyphics on the walls. "I wish I knew what these meant," she murmured.

Lex turned toward her, wide-eyed. "Th-those tell the mummy's legend," he stammered in a low voice.

"Legend?" Freddie's eyes lit up. "What kind of legend?"

Lex gulped. "Well, actually it's a poem, starting here." He pointed to the drawings and recited in a weak voice, " 'When the moon is full and the frost is near, Am-ho-tep will walk, so live in fear.' "

"Full moon? That's tonight," Freddie said.

"Lex, don't frighten the children," Mrs. Truesdale scolded.

"I'm only telling the legend." Lex gulped. "I've heard strange noises coming from that box." He stared at the casket and backed away again.

"I've never heard anything," Mrs. Truesdale said. "And Am-ho-tep has been in our family for over sixty years."

"It sounds like a fascinating story," Mrs. Bobbsey said brightly. "Do you mind if I include it in my article?"

Mrs. Truesdale glanced at Mr. Foxworth,

who smiled and shrugged. "All right." She sighed. "Who knows? A frightening story might lure more visitors to the exhibit."

Mr. Foxworth turned to Mrs. Bobbsey. "Would you like to take a picture of the mummy itself? I asked the men from the shipping company to stay and help us open the lid some more." He clapped his hands. "Joe! Carter!"

Two men in gray work clothes appeared in the doorway. As they approached the casket, everyone stepped aside—except Flossie.

She was staring at the mummy case. The painted carvings were so pretty, she thought. Maybe *she* should be a mummy for Halloween, too.

As the men lifted the lid, there was a low sound inside the casket, as if the dead king had taken a deep breath.

"Yeow!" Flossie jumped back. "I heard him!" she cried. "He made a sound!" She stumbled backward into Nan's arms.

"I knew it!" Lex turned to run, but his aunt grabbed his arm. "Can't I wait in the car?" he whimpered.

"No, you can't," Mrs. Truesdale said firmly. "This is ridiculous. It was probably only an echo."

"Or a rush of air," Nan added, hugging her shaking sister.

"I heard something," Flossie insisted. "Like he was—sighing!"

"Mummies do *not* sigh," said Mr. Foxworth with a sniff.

The others moved forward and stared down at the mummy. It looked like a big doll wrapped in ragged yellow cloth. It didn't move, and it didn't make a sound.

"There, you see?" Mrs. Bobbsey gave Flossie a reassuring squeeze. "Nothing to be afraid of."

"But I heard something," Flossie insisted. "I'm sure I did."

"I know." Freddie snapped his fingers. "The mummy said, 'Trick or treat.'"

While everyone laughed at Freddie's joke, Mrs. Bobbsey took photos of the mummy.

The man named Carter held up a pink slip of paper. "Mr. Foxworth, you have to sign this shipping order."

"Let's go to my office," Mr. Foxworth said. He turned to Mrs. Bobbsey. "We can finish the interview there. You kids may look around the museum if you like. But please be very careful. Don't touch!"

The four twins walked back down the

dimly lit hallway. Freddie lagged a little behind. What if the mummy *had* made a sound? he thought.

Freddie caught up to Flossie at the doorway to a large room filled with Greek pottery. "I'll be right back," he whispered to her. "Uh—I need to check something out for my costume."

While Nan and Bert peered at the Greek vases, Freddie quietly slipped back into the mummy's room.

A lone spotlight was focused on the open casket. The room was dead quiet.

Freddie tiptoed over to the casket and peeked in. Whew! Mummies really smelled musty.

Freddie leaned forward and reached out to touch the ragged bandages, but then he froze. The bandaged chest moved. Up, then down, then up again. The mummy was breathing.

Freddie tried to yell, but no sound came out. Then, before he could turn and run, the mummy's arms reached out to grab him!

2

A Living
Legend

Freddie found his voice. "He moved!" The mummy's arms dropped down to its chest, and Freddie raced for the hallway.

"It's alive! I saw it move!" Someone reached out of the shadows and grabbed him. Freddie screamed. Then he realized it was Bert.

"Take it easy. It's only me," Bert said.

"Flossie's right," Freddie said, panting. "The mummy's alive. He tried to grab me."

Bert glanced down the hall toward the mummy exhibit. "Come on. I've got to see this for myself."

"Wait up!" Nan called from behind them.

Flossie tugged on her big sister's sleeve. "I

told you," she said. "At least someone believes me now."

"I wanted to get another look," Freddie explained breathlessly. "I started to check out his bandages—for my costume—and he made a swipe at me."

When the Bobbseys entered the exhibition room again, Carter and Joe were there, lowering the lid on Am-ho-tep.

A man in a guard uniform waved a flashlight at the twins. "The museum is closed. What are you kids doing here?" he demanded.

"We're with our mother," Nan said. "She's writing a story on this mummy for the *Lakeport News*."

"Is that right? Well, we'd better go find her. I'm Mr. Morris, head of museum security, and I can't have you kids running around loose in here."

"But the mummy's alive!" Freddie blurted.

Carter and Joe looked at each other.

"Nonsense," Mr. Morris snapped. "This mummy is as dead as they come."

"You kids better beat it," Carter said.

"Yeah, or we'll let the mummy out," Joe added with a grin. "And he'll really chase after you."

"You don't have to tease Flossie and Freddie," Nan said, putting an arm on Freddie's shoulder. "They're already scared enough."

"That's no excuse for telling wild stories," Mr. Morris said. "Let's go, kids. You don't belong in here." He turned to the movers. "It's time you went, too."

The Bobbseys followed Mr. Morris out of the room. He pointed down the hall.

"Go straight to Mr. Foxworth's office," he ordered. "I have to let these men out." Angrily, Mr. Morris turned away.

"Boy, I wonder what's bugging him," Bert said.

Nan shrugged. "Maybe he's nervous. Or scared."

"Of what?" Bert said. "The mummy?" Bert made a ferocious face. He clawed the air, bared his teeth, and growled. Nan giggled, but the younger twins weren't amused.

"You wouldn't think it was so funny if you saw what I saw," Freddie said.

"You sure it wasn't a shadow?" Nan asked as they turned a corner.

Freddie shook his head. "The mummy raised his hands, I tell you." Freddie stuck his hands out in front of him like a zombie.

"Well, shadows don't make noises," Nan said. "But men lifting heavy objects do."

"Right," Bert said. "Flossie, are you sure you didn't hear Carter and Joe grunting when they picked up the lid?"

"The sound came from inside the box," Flossie insisted.

"Why didn't the rest of us hear the noise?" Nan questioned.

"I don't know," Flossie said. "Why won't you believe me?"

The Bobbseys reached the curator's office and paused in front of the door. They could hear their mother inside, talking to Mr. Foxworth.

"Let's ask Mom to drop us off at the library," Nan said. "Whether this mummy is alive or not, at least we can find pictures that could help with Freddie's costume."

It was a few minutes before seven when Mrs. Bobbsey parked in front of the Lakeport Public Library.

"If the photos I took of the mummy turn out well, this story could be on the front page." She smiled with pride.

"Terrific, Mom," Bert said as the twins climbed out of the car. "Maybe you'll want to use some of the information we dig up at the library."

"Good idea," Mrs. Bobbsey said. "But it's getting late. Please don't stay long."

"We won't," Bert called back. Then he hurried inside after the others.

The librarian led the twins to the section containing information on ancient Egypt and mummies. Eagerly, they began to comb through the books.

Nan found a chapter on Am-ho-tep.

"Look," she said. "He was buried in a pyramid more than three thousand years ago. And found by grave robbers in the 1920s. The robbers stole all of his jewels, gold-plated statues, ivory chests." She spread the book out on the table. "Oh, wow! No wonder Lex is so jumpy!"

"What did you find?" Bert asked.

"All the robbers died mysteriously! And the stolen treasure was never recovered. People believed that the mummy killed the thieves and that he won't rest until he gets his treasure back."

Bert recited the legend in a low voice. " 'When the moon is full and the frost is near, Am-ho-tep will walk, so live in fear.' "

"Ooh, Bert. That's creepy," Flossie said.

Freddie shivered and pushed an open book between the older twins. "Look at this picture."

The photo showed a mummy lying in a casket with his hands extended in front of him. The caption stated that the mummy was reaching for his next victim.

"That's what the mummy in the museum was doing," Freddie said. "I was going to be his next victim!"

"Let me see that." Bert flipped through the pages of the book, then he smiled. "These are movie mummies, not real mummies."

"Oh," Freddie said, disappointed.

"But look at this, Freddie." Bert held out another book. "This tells how to catch a mummy. You dig a shallow pit and line it with tanna leaves." He frowned. "What are tanna leaves?"

Nan shrugged. "Never heard of them."

" 'Tanna leaves will lure the mummy into the trap,' " Flossie read over Freddie's shoulder. " 'He needs them for sus . . . susten . . .' What's that word?" Flossie pointed.

" 'Sustenance,' " Nan said. "It means that the mummy needs the leaves to stay alive."

"Alive!" Freddie exclaimed. "I knew that mummy wasn't dead."

"It's just a silly legend," Nan said. "Mummies *are* dead. They can't eat anything."

The library lights blinked, and Freddie sighed. "The library is closing. Time to go."

Bert checked out the book that mentioned Am-ho-tep. He also checked out *The Complete Guide to Late-Night Movie Mummies.*

Outside, the sky was getting dark and the air was chilly. Since they were already late, the twins decided to take a shortcut through Lakeport Park.

"I don't know if this was such a good idea," Nan said. "It's pretty dark out." She shivered and reached for Flossie's hand.

"The moon will be up soon." Flossie tightened her grip on Nan's hand.

"Good point," Freddie said. "How does the legend go?" He pushed a low-hanging branch out of the way. "When there's a full moon and it's cold outside and—I'll bet the mummy wanted out tonight."

"Sure he did," Bert said. "If he isn't stiff from all that lying around." The older twins laughed.

"Did you hear that?" Flossie gasped. "Look at those bushes!"

They stared into the darkness. Something rustled in the leaves.

"Probably a rabbit," said Bert. He sounded nervous, though.

Nan looked at him. "Or it could be a squirrel," she said.

"Or it might be a mummy," Freddie added.

"It *is* a mummy," Flossie cried. "And there he is!"

3
Halloween Revelry

The mummy came right at them! His hands were stretched out in front of him. He was dragging his left foot and trailing his bandages in the dust. A tree limb swatted him in the face, and the mummy cried out in pain.

"He's h-howling!" Freddie stammered.

"Oh, no! He's headed this way," Flossie gulped.

Bert grabbed Freddie, and Nan took Flossie's hand. They ducked into the woods and ran as fast as they could. Thorny bushes slapped at their faces. They slipped on wet leaves and tripped over thick black roots.

When they reached the top of a low hill, they paused to catch their breath and glance back.

"Look!" Freddie exclaimed. "He's not following us."

The mummy had disappeared into the fog on the path below.

"What's that smell?" Nan asked. She pinched her nose.

"It's the mummy," Freddie said. "He smelled musty in the museum, too, after they opened his casket."

"Let's follow him," Bert said. He started down the hill.

Nan pulled her brother back. "We can't," she said. "It's getting late. Mom and Dad will wonder where we are."

The path was deserted, anyway. Bert agreed they'd better head home. Sticking close to the streetlights, they kept a lookout for the runaway mummy.

Mr. and Mrs. Bobbsey were waiting for the twins when they arrived.

"You should have been here ages ago," Mrs. Bobbsey said. Her eyes widened when she saw the stains and dirt on the twins' clothes. "What happened?"

"You won't believe it," Freddie said. "Remember how nobody believed Flossie and me when we saw the mummy move in the museum?"

"You kids have a great imagination," Mr. Bobbsey said. He ruffled Freddie's hair.

"It wasn't their imagination, Dad," Nan explained. "We saw the mummy in the park. He even chased us."

Quickly, she told her parents all about the bandaged figure stumbling through the fog.

"I know it sounds crazy," Nan said. "But it sure looked like Am-ho-tep."

"And smelled like him, too," Flossie said. She wrinkled her nose. "Phew."

Bert wanted to call the museum and ask if the mummy was missing, but Mrs. Bobbsey pointed out that the museum was closed.

"Besides, have you forgotten?" Mr. Bobbsey said. "It's only two days until Halloween. You might have seen someone coming home from a costume party."

"He looked awfully real," Flossie said.

"Well, what costume wouldn't look real on a foggy night like this?" Mrs. Bobbsey smiled. "He probably thought you kids were a bunch of goblins."

"What about that awful smell?" Flossie asked.

Mrs. Bobbsey shrugged. "Maybe the costume was left in an attic over the summer."

"I suppose it's possible," Nan said thoughtfully. "I guess we can't do anything about it now, anyway."

"But there's a mummy out there," Freddie protested.

"We'll check it out in the morning," Bert promised. "For now, let's get some sleep."

"*You* sleep," Freddie grumbled. "I'm keeping an eye out for mummies."

At the breakfast table the next morning the twins had just begun to discuss the mummy when a news bulletin came on the radio.

"The Lakeport Museum was robbed late last night," the announcer said. "An Egyptian mummy lent to the museum by Mrs. Eleanor Truesdale is missing. The head of security, Mr. Albert Morris, was found unconscious, next to the empty sarcophagus. Lakeport police are investigating. More news as it develops."

"Mr. Morris!" Nan cried. "He's the man we met yesterday."

"I bet that's our mummy—the one we saw in the woods," Freddie said. "But he wasn't stolen—he escaped."

"What was he doing in the woods?" Bert looked doubtful.

"Looking for tanna leaves," Flossie said. She looked down at her cereal. "Believe me, Crunchy Snaps look a whole lot better."

" 'When the moon is full and the frost is near, Am-ho-tep will walk, so live in fear,' " Bert teased Freddie.

"There *was* a full moon last night. And look!" Freddie tapped the windowpane. "There's frost on the ground this morning."

"Instead of arguing about it, maybe we could help the police," Nan said. "Let's go see Lieutenant Pike."

The Bobbseys had helped the lieutenant on many of his cases.

"Okay," Bert agreed. He stood up and saluted. "The Bobbsey Mummy Patrol is on its way."

To the twins' surprise, the police station was noisy and crowded with people. Nan counted twelve people who claimed to have seen the mummy the night before. Lieutenant Pike came out of his office, saw the twins, and said, "Not you kids, too!"

The Bobbseys grinned. Lieutenant Pike led them into his office. He sat down behind his desk to take their statement. They told him what time they had been in the park and which way the mummy had run.

"He sort of disappeared into the fog," Freddie said.

"I wish I could do that this morning," Lieutenant Pike said. He waved a sheaf of papers. "I barely have enough men to check all these sightings."

"We'd be happy to help you, Lieutenant," Bert offered.

"Thanks, but whoever stole that mummy is still running around loose, and a person like that could be dangerous," the lieutenant warned.

"More dangerous than the mummy itself?" Nan asked.

"The mummy everyone claims to have seen could have been someone dressed up for Halloween." Lieutenant Pike closed his notebook. "If I find some joker wearing a really nifty mummy costume, I'm going to arrest him for disturbing the peace." He rocked back in his chair and laced his fingers behind his head.

Nan frowned. "We're almost positive the mummy in the park was the same one we saw in the museum," she said.

"I'll keep that in mind. And you kids keep

your eyes open." Lieutenant Pike rose to his feet and led the Bobbseys out of his office. "If you see anything else, be sure to call me."

The station house was still crowded, but a familiar face caught Flossie's eye.

"Look!" she exclaimed. "It's Mr. Morris." The head of museum security was coming out of another lieutenant's office. His head was wrapped in bandages, and there were dark circles under his eyes. The twins gathered around him.

"Are you all right?" Flossie asked.

"Do I look all right?" Mr. Morris snapped. "Wait a minute, you're those rowdy kids from the museum last night."

"That's right," Flossie said. "We're the Bobbseys."

"We're here to report a mummy sighting," Freddie said. "We saw him in the park."

"You saw the mummy?" Mr. Morris squinted his eyes and shook his head. "Oh, my head hurts!"

"Who hit you?" Bert asked.

With a frightened look, Mr. Morris bent down and whispered, "I told the police. They think I'm crazy." He took a deep breath. "The mummy did it!"

4

Hidden Treasure

"The mummy did it?" Bert and Nan stared in surprise.

"I knew he was alive," Freddie said gleefully.

"He's strong, too." Mr. Morris would have said more, but a police officer came to drive him home in a squad car.

"Poor Mr. Morris," Flossie said as the injured man left the station. "No one believes him, either."

"Well, we believe you now," Nan said.

Bert nodded in agreement. "Someone hit Mr. Morris. Either a real mummy—"

"Or someone dressed up as one." Nan finished the sentence for him. "That's the mystery."

"Whoever it was," Bert said, "maybe we should go back and search the park. That's the last place we saw the—whatever it was."

As the twins marched to the park, a brisk wind blew up. Orange and brown leaves swirled through the streets.

"We'd better hurry, before all the clues blow away," Bert said as they entered the park.

"What's that?" Nan pointed to a strip of yellow material that was caught on a thorn-bush.

"Looks like a piece of Am-ho-tep's bandages." Bert carefully untangled the cloth. He smelled it. "It's him, all right."

"Here's another one," Nan shouted. She ran to the path they had traveled the night before.

"Ooh, he should change his detergent," Flossie said.

"Yeah, he needs whiter whites," Freddie agreed. "Hey—there's another piece."

"There's a whole trail of bandages!" Nan exclaimed.

By the time they reached the other side of the park, they had ten scraps of mummy bandage. At the edge of the park, the clues vanished. There were no more scraps of cloth.

"Let's search the neighborhood," Bert said.

"Maybe we can figure out which way the mummy went."

After the twins had searched two side streets and found nothing, they headed in a third direction. Nan hurried ahead of the others. "Hey, everybody!" she called. "Here's another piece. He went this way."

Several blocks later, the scraps were fewer. The twins moved slowly, searching carefully to see which way the mummy had gone.

"Wait a minute," Bert said. "This is *our* neighborhood. You don't think . . ."

He and Nan exchanged a look.

"I sure do," Freddie cried. He snatched a scrap of linen from the Bobbseys' own lawn. "The mummy was here last night. He followed us home!"

Flossie pulled a last piece of mummy cloth from their back door.

"I'm getting a shovel," Freddie announced.

"What for?" Bert said as he and the girls followed Freddie to the garage.

Freddie looked at Bert as if he were crazy. "To dig a mummy trap! The next time he comes around, we'll be ready for him."

"I'll gather leaves," Flossie offered. "We don't have real tanna leaves so oak leaves will have to do."

Bert rolled his eyes and walked over to Nan, who was studying a handful of crumbling mummy scraps.

"Let's take this material to Mr. Foxworth at the museum." Nan tucked the scraps into her pocket. "He'll know if they're real or fake."

"You don't believe in walking mummies, do you?" Bert asked.

"Right now I don't know what to believe," Nan said.

Nan and Bert jumped on their bikes and headed for the museum.

"Thanks for bringing these pieces of cloth to me." Mr. Foxworth peered through a magnifying glass as Bert looked over his shoulder. "But they definitely don't belong to Mrs. Truesdale's mummy."

Mr. Foxworth rubbed the cloth between his fingers. "I'm afraid you've been tricked. You saw someone dressed for a Halloween party."

Nan was about to leave when an open book on Mr. Foxworth's desk caught her eye. The book showed a large photo of a mummy that looked exactly like Am-ho-tep.

"How can you tell the age of the cloth without testing it?" Nan asked.

Mr. Foxworth slammed the book shut

when he saw the twins staring at the picture. He stacked all the books and papers on his desk and dropped them into a drawer.

"I can determine the material's age by its weave and feel," Mr. Foxworth told them. "This fabric was woven by a modern machine. It's too tight to have been done by hand."

"It smells as if it hasn't been washed for a million years," Bert said.

Mr. Foxworth sniffed the cloth. "It smells bad, but it's not from a mummy. It's a fake. I'm sure of it."

The curator glanced at his watch. "Now, have you any other questions?"

"I guess not," Nan said. She stood up.

"Thanks for your help," Bert told Mr. Foxworth.

As they went into the hall, Nan tugged on her brother's arm.

"Get him out of the office," she whispered to Bert. "I want a look at that book."

Bert thought fast. He stuck his head back in the curator's office. "Um, could you take me to the exhibition hall for a minute?" he asked. "I think I lost my comb last night outside the mummy's room."

Mr. Foxworth sighed. "Oh, very well. Let's

check at the lost-and-found desk first. Follow me."

"I think I'll wait here," Nan said. She sat down on a couch in the empty reception room.

Mr. Foxworth glanced at his office door, then looked at Nan. "All right. We'll be right back," he said.

Nan waited a minute, then slipped into Mr. Foxworth's office. She pulled open the bottom desk drawer and found the book she wanted.

It had a red cover and was entitled *Mummies of Ancient Egypt*. Nan found a section on Am-ho-tep. One sentence was underlined in red ink: "Recently discovered documents support the theory that Am-ho-tep was buried wearing a fortune in jewels."

Jewels! Nan gasped. The book said the mummy had them under his wrappings. No wonder the mummy had been stolen.

Lost in thought, Nan closed the book. She was about to drop it back in the drawer when a hand reached out of nowhere and grabbed her wrist.

"Here—let me help you," a deep voice said.

5

Secrets in the Leaves

Nan gasped. Her heart pounded as she whirled around. It was Mr. Morris. His head was still wrapped in bandages.

"Uh, I was just reading this book," Nan said quickly.

Mr. Morris frowned at her. "Let's see what Mr. Foxworth thinks about that," he said.

"Okay." With her free hand, Nan scooped up a few mummy scraps from the desktop as Mr. Morris pulled her to the door. Bert and Mr. Foxworth were coming up the hall.

"I caught her at your desk," Mr. Morris said to the curator.

"What were you doing there, young lady?" Mr. Foxworth's face went red with anger.

"I—I forgot these." Nan opened her hand, revealing the pieces of cloth.

Bert had an idea. "Maybe these scraps came from the mummy who knocked you out, Mr. Morris."

"That's nonsense." Mr. Morris shook his head. "I don't know what you're talking about. How could a mummy knock me out?"

Nan's eyes widened. "But you said—"

"I think you kids had better go home." Mr. Morris motioned to the door. "And if you're smart, you'll leave the investigating to the police," he added.

As they rode home on their bikes, Nan told Bert about the mummy's jewels. When they pulled into the driveway, they found the younger twins spreading handfuls of yellow leaves in a pit next to the garage.

"This is our mummy trap. Neat, huh?" Freddie boasted.

"The mummy will fall right in," Flossie said. "The leaves are for bait."

"They look just like the ones in the picture, even if they aren't genuine tanna leaves." Freddie brushed the dust off his jeans. "Do you think the mummy will know the difference?"

"Hardly." Bert stepped closer to the small

pit and then backed away. His shoes were caked with mud.

"We filled the hole with water," Flossie explained. "Mummies like things swampy."

Bert groaned. "Dad is going to kill you."

"Let me tell them what we've learned," Nan said. "Mr. Foxworth said the mummy in the park was a fake."

"What?" Freddie and Flossie said together.

Nan explained about the red-covered book and the jewels hidden inside the mummy. She told him Mr. Foxworth had tried to keep her from seeing the book he was reading.

"Maybe Mr. Foxworth took the jewels," Freddie suggested.

"Or Mr. Morris," Bert said. "He lied about the mummy." He told the younger twins how the guard had said it wasn't a mummy that had hit him.

Nan shook her head. "I think he lied because he's afraid. He already said no one would believe him."

"Anyway, it's Mrs. Truesdale's treasure," Bert added. "Don't forget, she owns the mummy."

"Right. Let's ask her if she knows about the jewels."

"We can visit her after lunch," Freddie said. "I'm starved."

An hour later, all four twins jumped on their bikes. It was a long ride out to the Truesdale mansion. The narrow country road twisted through the wooded hills along the lake.

Bert pedaled his bike up beside Nan's. "Don't look now, but there's a car following us. An old, beat-up white Chevy," Bert said.

Nan stole a glance over her shoulder. "Can you see who's driving?"

"No—the car's not close enough," Bert answered.

The Truesdale mansion loomed ahead of them. It looked like an old castle. It had a steep roof with four round turrets, like towers.

"Spooky." Flossie shivered. "It looks like Frankenstein's castle."

"Too bad I didn't wear my costume," Bert joked.

The twins parked their bikes beside two marble lions. They climbed a flight of stone stairs. At the top of the stairs, Bert turned and checked the driveway for the beat-up white Chevy. It was nowhere in sight.

An elderly butler led the Bobbseys into a

huge arched entryway. "Wait here, please." He went to find the Truesdales.

Flossie stared at a suit of armor guarding the staircase. "Maybe the mummy is hiding in there," she said.

"Ssh." Nan grabbed her elbow. "I hear voices."

"I don't want to talk to them." It was Lex's voice. He sounded scared.

"But they just want to help find Am-ho-tep," Mrs. Truesdale replied.

"I don't want to find him," Lex whined. "Or his curse."

Two huge doors swung open, and Mrs. Truesdale and Lex entered the room.

"Hello, children," she said sweetly.

Nan showed Mrs. Truesdale the scraps of mummy wrappings. She told her about seeing the mummy in the park. "Of course, we reported it to the police," Nan added.

Lex turned pale. "It's the curse! Am-ho-tep will haunt us for the rest of our lives!"

"Lex, don't be silly." Mrs. Truesdale turned to the twins. "Have you learned anything else?"

Nan told her about Mr. Foxworth's red-covered book and the hidden jewels. Freddie and Flossie described their mummy trap.

Mrs. Truesdale looked thoughtful. "I'll have to call Mr. Foxworth about those jewels. This is the first I've heard of them."

"We'll keep you posted," Nan promised.

Lex held the door open for them.

"Don't come back here," he whispered. "It's—it's not safe. The mummy might be after you." With a nervous wave, he closed the heavy door behind them.

"He sure doesn't want us to find Am-ho-tep," Freddie said.

"He's a scaredy-cat." Flossie jumped on her bike.

"Or maybe he's hiding something," Bert said. "Lex sure wanted to get rid of that mummy. Maybe he paid someone to do it for him. Maybe it wasn't a real theft at all."

The ride home was quiet. Each twin was lost in thought.

Suddenly a growling noise caught Bert's attention. "Wait—what's that?" he cried.

Before anyone could answer, a ghostly white figure leapt out of a clump of bushes. It flung a stick into the spokes of Bert's bike, then turned and ran away.

"Stop that mummy," Nan cried.

6

Trick-or-Treat Terror

Pling! The fat stick wedged itself between two spokes and then jammed against the bike's fender. The front wheel locked, and Bert went flying over the handlebars.

He landed on the gravel, skinning his hands. His bike crashed in a heap behind him.

Nan swerved to avoid hitting him. Her bike slid out from under her, and she fell, too. The younger twins barely stopped in time to avoid running into Nan and Bert.

"Are you all right?" Nan ran over to her brother.

"A couple of scratches," Bert said. "At least I didn't tear my jeans. Where'd the mummy go?"

"He ran back into the woods," Freddie said. "Look at the stick he threw into your spokes." Freddie pointed. "There's something wrapped around it."

Freddie pulled the stick out of the wheel's spokes. A piece of paper was attached to the stick with rubber bands. Freddie rolled the rubber bands off the stick and unwrapped the yellowish paper. He held the paper in front of him so that they could all see it. The paper was covered with squiggly symbols and tiny pictures of animals.

"Mummy talk," said Flossie.

"Let me see the note," Nan said. Freddie handed her the paper. "These symbols look familiar." She frowned. "I know! They're hieroglyphics like the ones in Am-ho-tep's tomb."

"I'll bet it's the curse," Freddie said. "No wonder Lex is afraid. Now the curse is on us."

"Only receiving the curse means we're getting close to finding out what happened to the museum mummy," Bert pointed out. "Someone has gone to a lot of trouble to stop us."

"Bert's right," Nan said. "That was no escaped mummy. Whoever threw that stick was here for one reason—to scare us."

Freddie looked disappointed. "It could have been a real mummy."

"I don't think so." Nan frowned. "Someone must have known we'd be on this road—but who?"

"We have one suspect," Bert said. "The driver of the car that was following us."

Bert checked his bike to make sure the wheel would still spin. It was fine.

Flossie looked at the woods nervously. "This place is spooky. Can we go before that mummy comes back?"

"Okay." Nan sighed. "We can think about this better at home."

"You can say that again," Freddie murmured.

Bert led the way, and they made it home in record time. As soon as they got there, the younger twins parked their bikes in the garage and ran into the backyard to check on their mummy trap. No luck—it was empty. But stuck in the soft mud next to the mummy trap was a stick Freddie had never seen before. Attached to the stick was a piece of white paper. There was writing on it.

"What's this?" Freddie's voice cracked with excitement. He stooped down and pulled the

note off the stick. Flossie leaned over his shoulder, breathing into his face.

"Another mummy note?" she asked.

Freddie's face fell. "Aw—no such luck," he told his sister. "It's from Dad. He slipped on this mud. He says he doesn't know what we're up to, but we have to fill in this hole right away, so that none of the trick-or-treaters will get hurt on Halloween night."

"Halloween is tomorrow night," Flossie murmured. "I'll bet that's exactly when the mummy will show up here."

"We'll just have to catch him before then." Freddie looked determined as he and Flossie joined Nan and Bert. "Do you think we can, Nan?" Freddie turned to his older sister.

"Can what?"

"Catch the mummy before tomorrow night."

"I don't know," Nan answered. "But let's take another look at that note—the one from the mummy."

"Looks like computer paper." Leaning close to Nan, Bert pointed to the sides of the note.

"Right," Nan agreed. "You can just see where the holes were torn off. But the edges have been burned. I think someone used a flame to yellow the paper to make it look older."

"Maybe this will help the police," Bert said. "But they'll find only our fingerprints on it. The mummy's hands were all bandaged."

Later that evening Nan and Bert held a meeting in Bert's bedroom. While Bert sat at his desk to take notes on the case, Nan stretched out on the bed.

She told him about her call to the police. Lieutenant Pike had been out. A Detective Peters had told her he was sure the lieutenant would want to see the letter written in hiero-glyphics.

"Did you tell him about the white Chevy that followed us to the Truesdale mansion?" Bert asked.

"He said there wasn't much he could do without a license-plate number or a descrip-tion of the driver."

Bert sighed. "If only the car had gotten closer." He looked down at the notepad on his desk. "As far as I can tell, we should be con-centrating on Lex and Mr. Foxworth. Lex is acting the weirdest, but Mr. Foxworth has the strongest motive for stealing the mummy."

"Could Lex have thrown that stick in your spokes?" Nan wondered. She propped her head up with her hand. "I mean, after we left his house, would he have had enough time to change into a mummy costume and sneak down the hill behind us?"

"I don't think so," Bert said. "Of course, Lex would know those hills around the Truesdale estate better than we do. There might be a shortcut through the woods or even a secret tunnel."

Bert drummed his pencil on the desk. "I've got a hunch that car following us has something to do with the missing mummy."

"Maybe that's how the mummy disappeared so quickly after he knocked you off your bike," Nan said. "Someone could have picked him up in that Chevy."

"No one would think it was strange to see someone riding around dressed as a mummy on the day before Halloween," Bert agreed.

"Okay, then, what about Mr. Foxworth?" Nan asked. "He would know how to wrap a mummy," she said. "But he didn't know we were going to Mrs. Truesdale's."

There were footsteps on the stairs and loud voices. The door to Bert's room flew open, and Freddie and Flossie bounded in. They were dressed in their pajamas, but instead of getting ready for bed, they were arguing loudly.

"He was tall and skinny," Freddie shouted.

"No, he wasn't," Flossie insisted. "He was fat! His belly stuck out to here." She held her hand a few inches in front of her stomach.

"I saw him first," Freddie said, "so I ought to know what he looks like."

"Well, maybe he went on an eating binge," Flossie said. She pouted, her hands on her hips.

Freddie slapped a hand over his eyes and groaned. "Tell her, Nan," he pleaded. "Am-ho-tep's as tall as a basketball player. He's as skinny as a rail."

"That was how he looked in the park," Nan agreed.

"But not today," Bert said. Frowning, he raked his fingers through his brown hair. "Now that you mention it, Flossie, he *was* kind of fat."

"See?" Flossie looked smug.

"Hold on," Nan said. "You both could be right."

Flossie glanced at her sister. "How?"

Nan grinned. "Simple. What if there are *two* mummies?"

Freddie gasped. "Two mummies! But that doesn't—"

He was interrupted by a loud shriek.

"Eeeiaahh!" someone cried. *"Owooiee!"*

Flossie jumped, looking frightened. "What was *that?*"

"It came from the backyard." Freddie raced to the window. Flossie followed him. Nan and Bert crowded in behind them.

They saw someone lying flat on his back next to the muddy mummy trap. Someone wrapped in white bandages.

Freddie jumped up and down. "He slid on the mud! He's in the trap!"

"It worked," Flossie shouted. "We caught a mummy!"

7

On the Mummy Watch

The twins ran down the stairs, Freddie and Flossie in the lead. "It worked! It worked!" the younger twins chanted.

Freddie was the first one through the back door, with Flossie close behind him.

But before they were halfway across the yard, the twins could see that the muddy trap was empty.

"Oh, no!" Freddie's shoulders sagged in disappointment. "He got away."

Flossie sighed. "It was probably the leaves. We should've used real tanna leaves."

"Wait a minute." Bert knelt down beside the muddy hole. He picked up something half covered with mud. "It's a watch. A man's—and very dirty." Bert shook it and held it up to his ear.

"Still running," he said. "None of us lost it, right?

Freddie and Flossie shook their heads.

"Me, neither," Nan said. "So it has to belong to whoever—whatever—was in the trap. Hold on while I get a flashlight—we can take a closer look."

Nan ran into the garage. She came back with the flashlight and shined the beam on Bert's hand.

"Why would a mummy need a watch?" Freddie asked.

"Good question," Nan said. "But if we find the man who lost this watch, we'll know who's parading around wrapped up like a mummy."

"Great," Bert said. "Exactly how are we going to do that?"

He and Nan stared at each other. Neither of them had an answer.

"What are you kids doing out there?" Mrs. Bobbsey called from the back porch. "Come back inside before you catch cold."

* * *

After breakfast the next morning, Bert set the watch in the center of the kitchen table.

"It's a Bullox," Bert said. "You know, those watches that take a lot of abuse."

" 'Shockproof, waterproof, scratch resistant,' " Flossie recited.

"And mummy-proof," Freddie joked.

"Whatever it is, the owner will be looking for it," Nan said, "and we have no idea who that is."

There was silence as the twins tried to figure out what to do next.

Nan snapped her fingers. "I have an idea. Where's the newspaper?"

Flossie fetched it for her. "Here—but what good is this?" Flossie looked puzzled. "Does the paper have a lost-and-found section?"

Nan held up the front page. She smiled happily. "It has something better," she told Flossie. "Look!"

Nan laid the paper on the table. On the front page was one of the photos Mrs. Bobbsey had taken at the museum.

"Mom's photo—remember?" Nan pointed. "She took a picture of the mummy in his casket."

Everyone crowded close to peer at the picture.

"Wait," Bert said. He whipped out his Rex Sleuther magnifying glass. "Let's use this." He studied the photo.

"Can I see?" Nan took the magnifying glass from Bert and leaned over the paper. She pointed to a wrist in the photo. "Look! The watch!"

Bert grabbed the magnifying glass. "But whose wrist is it?"

The photo showed two pairs of hands resting on the edge of the casket. There were no faces in the picture. It was impossible to guess whom the hands belonged to.

"This doesn't tell us anything!" Freddie wailed.

"Don't give up," Nan said, trying to keep everyone calm. "We have to try to remember who was there when Mom took this photograph."

The twins thought hard. "Well, Mr. Foxworth was there, and Lex, and Mrs. Truesdale . . ." Bert said.

"Mrs. Truesdale wouldn't wear a man's watch," Flossie said.

"You never know. She has big wrists," Nan pointed out. "She might wear a man's watch. That should be a lesson for you, Flossie—a

good detective never rules out any suspect without evidence."

"But these wrists are hairy," Flossie said, pointing to the photo. "Much hairier than Mrs. Truesdale's."

Nan smiled sheepishly. "You're right, Floss. Guess I owe you an apology."

Flossie looked proud of herself.

"At least we've eliminated one suspect," Bert said. "Now, who else was in the room when the casket was opened?"

"Those moving men were there," Freddie said eagerly.

"Okay—those are all our suspects." Bert turned toward Nan.

"Right," Nan said. "But now we need evidence. Let's call Mrs. Truesdale. I'll tell her we've found Lex's watch and see what she says."

The Bobbseys all agreed. Nan looked up Mrs. Truesdale's name in the phone book and dialed her number.

"Oh, my word, no," Mrs. Truesdale said when Nan described the stainless-steel watch. "Lex wears a very thin gold watch. And he hasn't lost it."

Nan thanked her and hung up. "Lex is out,"

she said. "Three suspects to go—Foxworth, Carter, and Joe."

"We'd better go to the museum right after lunch," Bert suggested. "Tonight's Halloween. We don't have much time to wrap this case up."

"Yeah—and I have to be home in time to wrap *myself* up," Freddie said. "As a mummy, that is."

Flossie knocked on the door of Mr. Foxworth's office.

"Oh, Flossie Bobbsey. What can I do for you?" Mr. Foxworth got to his feet.

"It's this mummy writing," Flossie said. "Could you tell me what it means?" She handed him a copy of the note that had been stuck in Bert's bicycle wheel.

"Let me see." He took the paper. "Hmm, well." He peered at her over the top of his reading glasses. "I know where you got this."

"You do?" Flossie's blue eyes were wide.

Mr. Foxworth smiled. "These are the same hieroglyphics that are on the walls of the exhibition room. You made a copy."

Mr. Foxworth leaned forward, resting his arms on his desk. His shirtsleeves covered his wrists. Flossie couldn't tell if he was wearing a watch or not.

"Yes," Mr. Foxworth continued, "these are from the tomb. The Egyptians put these threats on the walls of all their tombs, to keep out grave robbers." He sighed. "But you see, it didn't work this time. Our tomb was still robbed. So you have nothing to be afraid of."

"Don't feel too bad," Flossie said. She reached out and patted Mr. Foxworth's left arm. As she patted, she pushed his cuff back. There was his watch!

"Thank you, Flossie." Mr. Foxworth took off his glasses and rubbed his eyes. "These things happen, I guess. They've just never happened here before."

"Don't worry, Mr. Foxworth," Flossie said. "We'll find the robbers for you."

Mr. Foxworth didn't seem to believe her, but he smiled, anyway. He shook Flossie's hand. "You do that," he said.

Freddie, Bert, and Nan were waiting for Flossie in the hallway when Mr. Morris came by.

"Shouldn't you kids be home, getting ready for Halloween?" he asked.

"I guess so," Bert said. "Uh, could you tell us what time it is, please?"

Mr. Morris pulled up his sleeve and glanced at his watch. "Two-fifteen."

"Oh, Mr. Morris—is that today's paper?" Nan asked.

"Sure is." Mr. Morris pulled a folded newspaper out from under his arm. "You probably want to show me the picture your mother took. Not bad," he said. He pointed to the photo. "Too bad you can't see the faces— you'd never know it was a photo of Carter and Joe."

"The men from the shipping company?" Nan smiled sweetly. "Bert, why don't we take a copy over there and show it to them?"

"That's a nice idea, kids. Wait. I'll write down the address." Mr. Morris scribbled on a piece of paper and handed it to Nan. "I'll call and tell them you're coming," he said.

"Oh, don't do that," Nan said quickly. She exchanged a look with the other twins. "We want this to be a surprise."

8

A Muddy Trail

"Stand still, Freddie," Mrs. Bobbsey ordered. She held a pincushion and scissors. "I have to make some changes. Your costume keeps unraveling."

Freddie squirmed. He was tired of standing on the kitchen stool. His mother pinned a loose strip of white cloth to his white pants leg.

"How does this look?" Flossie held up a glittery bracelet. She slid it onto her wrist and held it out so her mother could see.

"My bracelet?" Mrs. Bobbsey looked startled. Then she rolled her eyes. "Okay, I guess you can wear it, Flossie. It looks very nice."

Flossie smiled happily. "I look like a very

glamorous cat," she said, drawing out the long word.

"Nice costume, Floss," Bert said. Dressed like Frankenstein, he clomped into the kitchen in heavy black boots. Mr. Bobbsey used the boots every day at his lumberyard. He had loaned them to Bert for Halloween.

"Heee, heee, heee," someone screeched. A horrible head poked inside the doorway. It had a long, crooked, warty nose and a pointed chin. The head was topped by a tall black hat.

"Hi, Nan," Bert teased. "Are you wearing a mask? Or is that the real you?"

"Watch out." Nan cackled. "Or I'll cast an evil spell on you."

"I'll be careful," Bert said. He turned to Mrs. Bobbsey. "Is Freddie ready yet?" he asked. "We have to get to the Acme Shipping Company before it closes."

"Yes, to return the watch," Nan added. "We want to do it before we go out trick-or-treating. We don't have much time."

Mrs. Bobbsey glanced at a photo of Am-ho-tep. It was propped against the napkin holder on the kitchen table. Freddie was starting to look exactly like the mummy.

"Well, if you want to get there before closing time, I'm afraid Freddie will have to stay behind," their mother said.

Freddie groaned. "I miss all the fun."

"If you want a great costume for tonight, you'd better stay," Mrs. Bobbsey said firmly.

"We'll be back in an hour—or less," Nan promised.

Flossie teased. "Don't worry, Freddie—I'll tell you all about it."

Freddie pulled her tail, and Flossie squealed.

"Stop that, Freddie. If we finish sooner, I'll drop you off at the shipping company," Mrs. Bobbsey promised.

Freddie sighed. "All right. I guess I can meet them later." He turned toward his brother and sisters. "But don't solve any mysteries without me."

A little while later, Flossie, Nan, and Bert pulled their bikes into the noisy yard of the Acme Shipping Company. Large trucks backed up to loading docks while forklifts moved back and forth across the platform.

"There's the white Chevy that followed us to Mrs. Truesdale's!" Bert exclaimed. The car was parked near the entrance to the building.

"Hey! What are you kids doing here?" A

man shouted at them from the loading dock. "Isn't it a little early for trick-or-treating?" he teased them.

"We didn't come here for candy," Nan shouted back. "We're here to return something."

Bert shouted, "It belongs to one of the men who delivered the mummy to the Lakeport Museum." He pulled off his Frankenstein mask to get a better look around. "I think that's his car." Bert pointed at the Chevy.

The man signaled the twins to come up to the loading dock. They climbed up an orange metal ladder. The man smiled and introduced himself as Mel.

"We're looking for Carter and Joe," Bert explained. "The two guys who delivered the mummy."

"Two guys? I thought there were three on the museum job," Mel said. He scratched his head. "Well, I don't know. What are you returning?"

Bert looked at Nan, who nodded her head to let him know it was all right to tell.

"We found a watch," Bert said. He described it.

"That might be Carter's watch," Mel said. "Okay, follow me."

He led the twins to a flight of creaky wooden stairs. "Down here," he said.

They ended up in a dark, cool basement. There seemed to be many rooms coming off a long hallway. The hallway was dim and lined with wooden crates.

Nan nudged Bert. She pointed to some muddy footprints on the concrete floor. The mud was mixed with dried leaves and pieces of cloth. Nan bent down and pulled a cloth scrap out of the muck.

"Tanna leaves," Flossie gasped. "I mean, oak leaves—from our mummy trap."

"And the cloth is a mummy wrapping," Bert whispered back.

Ahead of them, Mel opened a door to a brightly lit room. It was full of vending machines and tables and chairs. "You can wait here," he said. "I'll be right back."

The twins sat down. As soon as Mel had left the room, Nan sprang up again.

"We have to follow those muddy footprints," she said.

"Mel told us to wait here," Flossie reminded her.

"But he might be the one who stole the mummy. And if he is, he could be setting a trap for us right now," Bert pointed out.

"Let's sneak out of here and see where those prints lead," Nan suggested. "Maybe we can get back before Mel does."

Bert crept to the doorway and checked the hall. It was empty. Signaling Nan and Flossie to follow, he retraced his steps back to the muddy prints. The trail led deep into the building.

"It's like a maze," Nan said, shining a flashlight on the floor.

They found themselves in a dark, dusty storage area. Boxes were piled everywhere. The noisy loading dock was at the other end of the warehouse. This room was very quiet.

Nan sniffed the air. "Do you smell that?" she asked.

Bert nodded. "Musty, like the mummy," he said.

"Sssh," Flossie whispered. "Listen to that— people arguing."

It sounded as if the people were coming right around the corner.

"I'm telling you, Ned, it's not my turn," a voice said. "I can't see out of that pile of rags, anyway."

"But Carter really messed up last night," another voice said.

"How was I supposed to know there'd be a

muddy hole next to their garage? I already lost my watch." Carter sneezed. "And I think I'm catching a cold, too." He sneezed again.

"Okay, Joe, it's your turn," Ned, the first man, said. "Carter's sick."

"Not me." Joe groaned. "I can barely fit into those rags."

Flossie squeezed between a stack of crates. "I can see who it is," she whispered.

Nan and Bert peered over Flossie's head. Carter, Joe, and the third man, Ned, were fighting over a mud-splattered mummy costume.

"Those are the guys who delivered the mummy, all right," Bert murmured. He pointed to Carter and Joe. "But who's the skinny guy?"

"He *was* the mummy!" In her excitement, Nan bumped her head against a crate.

"What was that?" asked Joe.

"Nothing. Take it easy," Carter said.

"I can't." Joe looked around. "It's Halloween." He swallowed nervously.

"Don't be stupid." Carter sneezed again. "Tonight's our last chance."

Somewhere, a heavy metal door slammed shut.

Joe jumped. "What was that?"

"Relax! Mel's probably locking up," Carter told him.

"I'd better check," Ned said. "We don't want to get locked in."

The Bobbseys couldn't see where Ned went.

"Let's get out of here," Nan whispered.

Slowly, the twins backed away from the crates.

"Don't take another step," a voice growled. It was Ned, and he was standing right behind them. "You kids aren't going anywhere!"

9

The Big Shadow

"Joe! Carter! Look what we've got here!" Ned shouted. He glared at the Bobbseys. "I guess we didn't scare you enough."

Joe and Carter ran around the stack of crates.

"What are you kids doing here?" Joe asked in surprise.

"We came to return this watch." Bert held it up.

"That's mine." Carter looked surprised, too. He took the watch out of Bert's hand.

"And we came for the mummy," Nan said.

Flossie stepped forward. "If you give back the mummy, we won't tell anyone you took it." She smiled brightly at Joe, who was the kindest-looking man.

"But we can't give it back," Joe whimpered. "I wish we could. I'm afraid of the curse."

"I tell you there is no curse," Carter said. He didn't look too sure, though. He ducked behind Joe, as if to make certain no mummy could ever find him. Suddenly none of the men looked so frightening anymore.

"I'm sure you have nothing to worry about," Nan said. "Not if you tell us where the mummy is."

"You can't save us," Joe said. "You're just a bunch of kids. We didn't mean to hurt the mummy, but now everything's gone wrong."

"Joe's right," Carter said. "We're very good moving men. I don't know how we dropped it."

"You *dropped* the mummy?" Nan stared. Bert looked at her and Flossie.

"Poor Am-ho-tep," Flossie said.

"We dropped him, and he just broke," Ned said sadly. "Into pieces—he's wrecked now."

"Wrecked," Carter said.

"Wrecked," Joe repeated.

For a minute, no one said anything.

"We wanted to confess," Ned said. "But you kids ruined that."

"How did we ruin it?" Nan was puzzled.

"We saw you and got scared." Ned still

looked scared. "We all drove to Mrs. Truesdale's in Joe's Chevy," he began.

"The white car that followed us!" Freddie exclaimed.

Ned nodded. "That's right—we saw you kids on the road. We were going to tell Mrs. Truesdale the truth—that we broke her mummy."

Joe cut in. "I even wore the mummy costume, to show her how we tried to fool everyone. But then we saw you, and we figured *you* were going to tell her about the mummy moving. I was scared—I thought you'd guessed something was wrong. I thought maybe you even knew it was me pretending to be the mummy."

The Bobbseys stared at Joe.

"We didn't know that—not then, anyway," Nan told Joe.

Bert's eyes lit up. "Then it was you who threw the stick at my bike," he cried.

Joe nodded.

"To scare you away," Carter said roughly. "You're awfully nosy kids."

"We didn't mean to do anything bad." Ned's eyes were pleading. He explained how they had been moving the casket from the truck to the museum loading dock.

"We took the cover off the casket to make it easier to lift."

"But the casket slipped, anyway," Joe said, "and the mummy fell out in the truck—and broke!"

"We were very scared," Ned admitted. "Am-ho-tep is priceless. We could never replace him."

"We were afraid we'd get fired," Carter added. "So we decided Ned would dress up as the mummy. We told Foxworth we had to go back to the warehouse for some equipment. When we got there we wrapped Ned up like a mummy. Then we drove back to the museum. Once everyone had seen the mummy, we sneaked Ned out."

"You were the skinny mummy." Flossie pointed at Ned.

"That's right. But I didn't do a very good job. You heard me breathing, and your brother saw me move."

Nan nodded thoughtfully. "So you all took turns being the other mummies—the one who followed us in the park and the one who threw the stick in Bert's spokes . . ."

"And the one we caught in the mummy trap," Flossie finished.

"Hey, that's pretty clever of you!" Joe exclaimed. "What are you, detectives or something?"

The Bobbseys exchanged smiles. "As a matter of fact, we are," Nan said.

"No wonder we didn't fool you," Carter said. He told the twins why he and the others had tried to frighten them away. "We were afraid someone would believe Flossie and Freddie's story and figure out that we had ruined Am-ho-tep."

"But it wasn't a very good idea," Ned said. "Now everyone thinks the mummy was stolen. They think we're thieves!"

Joe wailed. "It's the curse! 'When the moon is full and the frost is near, Am-ho-tep will walk, so live in fear.'"

"We should've come clean from the start." Ned shook his head. "Maybe the people at the museum could have put the mummy back together."

"And then the mummy wouldn't be so mad at us," Joe said.

"Stop talking like that," Carter said. "We'll never admit we did it—never!"

"Ned thinks you should," Bert said bravely. "And I agree."

"Me, too," Nan and Flossie said together.

"And I say we can't. And we can't let you tell, either."

Carter, Ned, and Joe stood directly in front of the Bobbseys, blocking the way out. On every side, crates were stacked up to the ceiling. The Bobbseys were trapped.

"What are you going to do?" Flossie whispered.

"Our parents will be looking for us," Nan told the three men. "We told our mother we'd be back in less than an hour."

"By the time they find you, we'll be long gone." Carter pulled a large packing crate in front of the twins.

"Put them kids in this box," Carter ordered his friends. "And get me an address label. I'll bet these kids would like to visit the North Pole." He started laughing wildly. But as Carter laughed, a loud moaning sound filled the air.

"What's that?" Ned and Joe screamed. Carter stopped laughing. He looked nervous. The room got even darker. A huge shadow darkened the wall.

Joe gulped. "Don't look now," he croaked, "but it's Am-ho-tep!"

10

Mummy to the Rescue

The mummy's shadow waved its arms. It moaned again, loud and long.

Joe screamed. Ned jumped, then tripped over Joe. Carter dived right into a pile of boxes.

"Am-ho-tep walks," the mummy cried. His voice was creepy and scary.

Police sirens wailed in the distance.

"It's the cops!" Carter yelled. "Let's get out of here."

The three men turned to run. The mummy let out a terrible scream. Then he tumbled and fell—right into a pile of cartons. The mummy stuck up his bandaged head and howled.

Carter, Ned, and Joe screamed in terror. They ran—smack into the arms of the police. Two police officers handcuffed the three men and led them away. Lieutenant Pike stayed in the room with the Bobbseys.

"Good work," the mummy cried.

It was Freddie, wearing his mummy costume. He stood up in the pile of boxes. "Trick or treat!" he said.

"Freddie, where did you come from?" Flossie cried.

"That window, up there." He pointed at a high basement window.

"And your shadow came from the light on the ceiling." Bert was impressed.

"Neat, huh?" Freddie grinned. "It was sort of an accident. I crawled in the window to look for you. I didn't plan to fall."

"But how did you know where to look for us?" Nan asked.

"That was easy. When you guys didn't get home on time, Mom drove me over here. The warehouse was closed. Mom called Lieutenant Pike, and I snooped around. This was the only room with the lights on."

"Speaking of snooping," Bert said, "the real mummy ought to be around here someplace."

He moved a couple of crates and rolled a barrel to one side.

"Look over here," Nan called. "This must be what they made the mummy costume out of." She pulled a strip of yellowish cloth from a box labeled Medical Supplies. The date was from twenty years before.

"Twenty years in this basement?" Flossie wrinkled her nose. "No wonder they stink."

Mrs. Bobbsey and Mel ran into the room. "Are you all right?" Mrs. Bobbsey reached for the nearest twin—Flossie—and hugged her.

"We're a little dusty," Flossie said, brushing her cat tail.

"They look safe to me." Lieutenant Pike winked. "Weird, but safe."

"I searched all over for you kids," Mel scolded. "I figured you had left, so I locked up."

"Sorry," Nan said. "We were following a clue."

"I never would have looked in here." Mel shook his head. "This room hasn't been used for almost twenty years."

"Anyway, we caught the mummy thieves," Lieutenant Pike said. "They're probably confessing now."

"But they're not really thieves," Nan said.

"They didn't mean to hurt the mummy," Flossie added. "It was an accident."

"If that's the case, then I'm sure Mr. Fox-worth will go easier on them." Lieutenant Pike wrote down what Flossie had said in his notebook.

"One thing bothers me, though." Lieutenant Pike scratched his head in confusion. "They kept begging my men to lock them up. They said this place is haunted."

"It is," Flossie said. "By Freddie."

Freddie held his arms out straight. Everyone laughed as he imitated a mummy. Freddie laughed, too, and forgot to watch where he was going.

"Look out," Flossie cried.

Too late—Freddie walked into a pile of crates and knocked them over. The top crate spilled. Something dusty and smelly rolled onto the floor.

"What's that?"

Everyone gathered around.

"Oh, wow!" Bert exclaimed. "It's Am-ho-tep! It's the real mummy! They hid him in this box."

Everyone crowded around. Am-ho-tep, broken into several pieces, lay on the floor.

"He looks like Humpty Dumpty," Flossie

said. "You know, when they couldn't put him back together again."

"Don't touch anything," Lieutenant Pike ordered.

"Is that my mummy?" Mrs. Truesdale rushed into the room. Mr. Foxworth ran in behind her.

"Did you say you'd found Am-ho-tep?" Mr. Foxworth cried. He and Mrs. Truesdale were both out of breath.

"They didn't mean to steal him," Flossie told them. "It was an accident."

"Maybe so, but he's all broken." Mrs. Truesdale looked as if she was going to cry.

Lieutenant Pike placed a hand on her shoulder. "You'd better identify him . . . or it," he told Mrs. Truesdale.

"I couldn't bear to," she said. She turned to Mr. Foxworth. "Would you do it for me?"

Mr. Foxworth nodded and walked over to the broken mummy. He studied it for a minute.

"I knew it!" He nearly jumped up and down, he was so excited. He pushed his hand inside some of the mummy's rags.

"Oh, yuck." Freddie made a face. "Mummy's guts."

"Not quite." Mr. Foxworth held up a string of bright red beads.

Everyone gasped.

"Maybe this will make you feel better," Mr. Foxworth said to Mrs. Truesdale. He blew on the beads, and a cloud of dust flew away. The beads gleamed like rare jewels.

"What are they?" Nan's eyes were round with surprise.

"Rubies!" Flossie exclaimed. "Can I try them on?"

"I don't think so, Flossie," Mr. Foxworth said kindly. "These are the most perfect rubies I've ever seen. They must be worth a fortune."

"Then Am-ho-tep really was buried with his royal jewels," Nan said.

Flossie looked sad. "Poor Am-ho-tep. He'll never wear his jewels again."

"I don't know about that." Mr. Foxworth smiled. "I'm sure my people at the museum can put him back together again. Then we can display him with the necklace—that is, if Mrs. Truesdale will let us keep them for a while."

"I don't suppose there's any harm in that," Mrs. Truesdale said.

"You know, Mrs. Truesdale, those jewels

would never have been found if the movers hadn't dropped the mummy," Nan pointed out.

Mrs. Truesdale frowned. "That's true. And it proves they were telling the truth. They didn't mean to steal the mummy and his jewels at all."

"Of course not." Freddie grinned. "Nobody would. Don't forget, the mummy carries a curse."

"Not anymore, Freddie." Mr. Foxworth rested a hand on Freddie's head. "You forget— since the jewels have been found, the curse is no good."

"No good!" Mrs. Truesdale looked happier than the twins had ever seen her. "Well, my nephew Lex will certainly be glad to hear about that." She clapped her hands together.

"And now I have an announcement." Mrs. Truesdale cleared her throat. "I'd like to thank the Bobbsey twins for solving the mystery of my missing mummy. Why don't you all come to my house tonight for a special Halloween party?"

The Bobbseys cheered.

"But, Freddie, you have to promise me one thing," Mrs. Truesdale added.

"What's that?" Freddie asked.

"Please—could you find another costume? I've had my fill of mummies for one year."

"Sure." Freddie grinned. "I don't mind. We already have this case all wrapped up."

NANCY DREW® MYSTERY STORIES
By Carolyn Keene

	ORDER NO.	PRICE	QUANTITY
THE TRIPLE HOAX—#57	64278	$3.50	_____
THE FLYING SAUCER MYSTERY—#58	65796	$3.50	_____
THE SECRET IN THE OLD LACE—#59	69067	$3.50	_____
THE GREEK SYMBOL MYSTERY—#60	67457	$3.50	_____
THE SWAMI'S RING—#61	62467	$3.50	_____
THE KACHINA DOLL MYSTERY—#62	67220	$3.50	_____
THE TWIN DILEMMA—#63	67301	$3.50	_____
CAPTIVE WITNESS—#64	62469	$3.50	_____
MYSTERY OF THE WINGED LION—#65	62681	$3.50	_____
RACE AGAINST TIME—#66	62476	$3.50	_____
THE SINISTER OMEN—#67	62471	$3.50	_____
THE ELUSIVE HEIRESS—#68	62478	$3.50	_____
CLUE IN THE ANCIENT DISGUISE—#69	64279	$3.50	_____
THE BROKEN ANCHOR—#70	62481	$3.50	_____
THE SILVER COBWEB—#71	62470	$3.50	_____
THE HAUNTED CAROUSEL—#72	66227	$3.50	_____
ENEMY MATCH—#73	64283	$3.50	_____
MYSTERIOUS IMAGE—#74	64284	$3.50	_____
THE EMERALD-EYED CAT MYSTERY—#75	64282	$3.50	_____
THE ESKIMO'S SECRET—#76	62468	$3.50	_____
THE BLUEBEARD ROOM—#77	66857	$3.50	_____
THE PHANTOM OF VENICE—#78	66230	$3.50	_____
THE DOUBLE HORROR OF FENLEY PLACE—#79	64387	$3.50	_____
THE CASE OF THE DISAPPEARING DIAMONDS—#80	64896	$3.50	_____
MARDI GRAS MYSTERY—#81	64961	$3.50	_____
THE CLUE IN THE CAMERA—#82	64962	$3.50	_____
THE CASE OF THE VANISHING VEIL—#83	63413	$3.50	_____
THE JOKER'S REVENGE—#84	63426	$3.50	_____
THE SECRET OF SHADY GLEN—#85	63416	$3.50	_____
THE MYSTERY OF MISTY CANYON #86	63417	$3.50	_____
THE CASE OF THE RISING STARS—#87	66312	$3.50	_____
THE SEARCH FOR CINDY AUSTIN—#88	66313	$3.50	_____
THE CASE OF THE DISAPPEARING DEEJAY—#89	66314	$3.50	_____
THE PUZZLE AT PINEVIEW SCHOOL—#90	66315	$3.95	_____
THE GIRL WHO COULDN'T REMEMBER—#91	66316	$3.50	_____
NANCY DREW® GHOST STORIES—#1	46468	$3.50	_____

and don't forget...THE HARDY BOYS® Now available in paperback

Simon & Schuster, Mail Order Dept. ND5
200 Old Tappan Road, Old Tappan, NJ 07675

Please send me copies of the books checked. (If not completely satisfied, return for full refund in 14 days.)

☐ Enclosed full amount per copy with this coupon.
(Send check or money order only.)
Please be sure to include proper postage and handling:
95¢—first copy
50¢—each additonal copy ordered.

☐ If order is for $10.00 or more,
you may charge to one of the
following accounts:
☐ Mastercard ☐ Visa

Name _____ Credit Card No. _____

Address _____

City _____ Card Expiration Date _____

State _____ Zip _____ Signature _____

Books listed are also available at your local bookstore. Prices are subject to change without notice.

NDD-19

THE HARDY BOYS® SERIES
By Franklin W. Dixon

NIGHT OF THE WEREWOLF—#59	62480	$3.50
MYSTERY OF THE SAMURAI SWORD—#60	67302	$3.50
THE PENTAGON SPY—#61	67221	$3.50
THE APEMAN'S SECRET—#62	69068	$3.50
THE MUMMY CASE—#63	64289	$3.50
MYSTERY OF SMUGGLERS COVE—#64	66229	$3.50
THE STONE IDOL—#65	62626	$3.50
THE VANISHING THIEVES—#66	63890	$3.50
THE OUTLAW'S SILVER—#67	64285	$3.50
DEADLY CHASE—#68	62447	$3.50
THE FOUR-HEADED DRAGON—#69	65797	$3.50
THE INFINITY CLUE—#70	62475	$3.50
TRACK OF THE ZOMBIE—#71	62623	$3.50
THE VOODOO PLOT—#72	64287	$3.50
THE BILLION DOLLAR RANSOM—#73	66228	$3.50
TIC-TAC-TERROR—#74	66858	$3.50
TRAPPED AT SEA—#75	64290	$3.50
GAME PLAN FOR DISASTER—#76	64288	$3.50
THE CRIMSON FLAME—#77	64286	$3.50
SKY SABOTAGE—#79	62625	$3.50
THE ROARING RIVER MYSTERY—#80	63823	$3.50
THE DEMON'S DEN—#81	62622	$3.50
THE BLACKWING PUZZLE—#82	62624	$3.50
THE SWAMP MONSTER—#83	49727	$3.50
REVENGE OF THE DESERT PHANTOM—#84	49729	$3.50
SKYFIRE PUZZLE—#85	67458	$3.50
THE MYSTERY OF THE SILVER STAR—#86	64374	$3.50
PROGRAM FOR DESTRUCTION—#87	64895	$3.50
TRICKY BUSINESS—#88	64973	$3.50
THE SKY BLUE FRAME—#89	64974	$3.50
DANGER ON THE DIAMOND—#90	63425	$3.50
SHIELD OF FEAR—#91	66308	$3.50
THE SHADOW KILLERS—#92	66309	$3.50
THE BILLION DOLLAR RANSOM—#93	66310	$3.50
BREAKDOWN IN AXEBLADE—#94	66311	$3.50
DANGER ON THE AIR—#95	66305	$3.50
WIPEOUT—#96	66306	$3.50
CAST OF CRIMINALS—#97	66307	$3.50
SPARK OF SUSPICION—#98	66304	$3.50
THE HARDY BOYS® GHOST STORIES	50808	$3.50

NANCY DREW® and THE HARDY BOYS® are trademarks of Simon & Schuster, registered in the United States Patent and Trademark Office.

AND DON'T FORGET...NANCY DREW CASEFILES® NOW AVAILABLE IN PAPERBACK.

Simon & Schuster, Mail Order Dept. HB5
200 Old Tappan Road, Old Tappan, NJ 07675
Please send me copies of the books checked. (If not completely satisfied, return for full refund in 14 days.)

☐ Enclosed full amount per copy with this coupon
(Send check or money order only.)
Please be sure to include proper postage and handling:
95¢—first copy
50¢—each additonal copy ordered.

☐ If order is for $10.00 or more, you may charge to one of the following accounts:
☐ Mastercard ☐ Visa

Name _____ Credit Card No. _____

Address _____

City _____ Card Expiration Date _____

State _____ Zip _____ Signature _____

Books listed are also available at your local bookstore. Prices are subject to change without notice.

HBD-22